Tales from Panchatantra

Book-1

AF644311

DREAMLAND PUBLICATIONS

J-128, Kirti Nagar, New Delhi -110 015, India

Tel : +91-11-2510 6050, 2543 5657

E-mail : dreamland@dreamlandpublications.com

Shop online at www.dreamlandpublications.com

Follow us on www.instagram.com/dreamland.publications

UNION IS STRENGTH

Long ago, there lived a flock of parrots in a forest. Every day they used to fly far and wide in search of food. Before nightfall, they used to come back to their nests.

In the flock, there was an old parrot who was very wise. All the parrots used to respect him and follow his advice. One day, after flying a long distance, the parrots did not find any food. They felt exhausted and decided to rest for some time. But, the wise old parrot encouraged them to fly a little further.

After flying a little ahead, the smallest parrot looked down and saw plenty of corn grains scattered under a huge tree. He at once landed on the ground and all the parrots followed him except the wise old fellow. The old parrot sat on a branch of a nearby tree and tried to stop his friends.

But none of the parrots listened as they were hungry and tired as well. They did not see the hunter sitting on the tree, and all of them began to eat. Looking at the parrots busy enjoying their food, he cast a net over them.

The hunter was very happy to see so many parrots trapped in his net. Looking at the hunter coming down the tree, the parrots fluttered to free themselves but in vain. “What should we do now?” They all cried.

When he saw his fellow friends in trouble, the old wise parrot said, “Don’t lose courage. All of you pick up a part of the net and try to fly up together.” All the parrots did as told, and soon they were flying high carrying the net with them.

The hunter looked up in awe. He ran after the flying birds but could not catch them. The wise parrot took the entire flock to a place where his old friend, a rat, lived. Seeing the parrots trapped in the net, he immediately started nibbling at the net. Soon all the parrots were free.

The wise parrot said, “My friends if you stay united, you can do anything.” All the parrots thanked the rat and also thanked their wise old friend for their help.

Moral: Union is strength.

THE FOOLISH DONKEY

Once there lived a washerman in a village. He had a donkey who used to carry loads of dirty clothes to the river for washing and back home every day. Despite all his hard work, the washerman did not feed the donkey well.

So, at night the donkey wandered in the fields nearby and freely grazed on fresh crops to satisfy his hunger. One night, when the donkey was on his way to the fields, he met a fox. They soon became good friends and started meeting every night.

One day, the donkey said to the fox, "My friend, why don't you join me for dinner tonight! The field is full of juicy red tomatoes, let's go there and enjoy." The fox agreed, and both of them went to feast on the tomatoes.

Having eaten full, the donkey felt like singing, but the fox said, "No! No! Please don't sing. If you sing, the farmers of this field will wake up and catch us." The fox warned the donkey but the donkey ignored the fox and began to bray loudly.

Sensing danger, the fox immediately ran away and hid behind a huge tree. The donkey started braying on top of his voice. Listening to his voice, the farmers woke up and caught the donkey and thrashed him for eating tomatoes, and tied a heavy log to his neck.

Moral: There is time and place for everything. Think before you act.

TRUE FRIENDS

Once in a forest lived four friends – a mouse, a crow, a deer, and a tortoise. They were always seen together. One morning, a hunter came into the forest and laid a trap near the lake. Unfortunately, the deer had just reached the lake and so was caught in it.

Hearing the deer's cries, his friends came rushing there. The mouse started nibbling the cords of the net. The crow settled on a high branch of a tree nearby to keep a check on the hunter.

Soon, the deer was free from the trap. All the friends were overjoyed to be united. The crow saw the hunter approaching and alerted his friends. The deer hid behind the bush and the mouse darted into a hole nearby. But the tortoise, could not escape as fast as his friends and got caught.

The hunter picked up the tortoise and put him into his bag. Together, the three friends came up with a plan. The crow flew high up in the sky, and the deer ran ahead of the hunter. Keeping his bag on the ground, the hunter ran behind the deer.

The mouse cut the rope of the bag and set the tortoise free. The deer dodged the hunter and ran away. Disappointed, the hunter came back and found the bag open. The tortoise was also not there. The hunter had lost everything. He sadly left the place. The four friends were united again and lived happily in the forest.

Moral: True friends always help each other no matter the situation.

THE CROW LEARNT A LESSON

Once, there was a falcon and a crow. The crow was looking at the falcon and felt very happy to see the way it swooped down, lifted small creatures and then flew high up towards the sky leaving them. The crow started to practice like the falcon to sweep low and fly high. After some days, the crow felt confident to try his new skills. The crow now tried flying down like the falcon and then tried to fly up high, but in trying to imitate the falcon, the crow hit the ground and got bruised on its wings. After that day, the crow thought it was better to be original than copy others and harm oneself. The crow now mastered its own skills of flying and never copied any other birds in the neighbourhood.

Moral: Never copy others.

THE CAMEL AND THE BABY

One day, a camel and her baby talked to each other. The baby asked, "Mother, why do we camels have humps?" The mother replied, "Dear, our humps are for storing water, and we need this water to survive in the desert."

"Oh," said the baby. "We also have rounded feet. Why is this mother?" The camel said, "Our legs help us move around in the sand." Then the baby wanted to know why their eyelashes were long. The mother told him that their long eyelashes protect their eyes from dust.

The baby camel said, "So mother, we have humps to store water in the desert, rounded hooves to walk in the desert sand, and long eyelashes to protect us from the sand.

The mother camel said, "God has created everyone with unique features that help them survive, so we must be thankful."

Moral: Be thankful for everything you have.

BLUE-DYED JACKAL

A long time ago, there lived a jackal who strayed into a town in search of food. He accidentally entered a washerman's house. While trying to hide, the jackal slipped and fell into a tub full of blue-coloured dye. When the jackal entered the jungle, the animals did not recognise him, and they looked at him in awe and whispered to each other, "Who is this strange fellow?"

This made the jackal very happy. He told himself, "I can now easily fool anyone in the jungle." He said, "Hey animals! Don't be afraid. Lord of heaven has sent me to rule the jungle."

All the animals believed his words and made him the king of the jungle.

One day, the king jackal made an announcement, “I order all the jackals of this jungle to leave at once.” The jackal ordered such as he feared recognition.

A wise jackal among them said, “Friends, I smell a rat in the matter. The new king looks like us.”

The herd of jackals howled together. Unable to control his instinct, the blue jackal began to howl like other jackals.

All the animals heard him howling and shouted, “You cannot trick us anymore.” They chased him away from the jungle.

Moral: Do not pretend to be what you are not.

THE CAT AND THE ROOSTER

One day, a proud cat was arguing with a rooster. He told the bird, "You make such horrible noise. We are better off without you. Even the farmer has been complaining. You should go away so that all of us can sleep peacefully." The rooster replied, "No, I cannot, I wake all every morning so that they can work and earn a living. You keep sleeping lazily. It is only you who does not like me crowing."

The cat was surprised to see the rooster talk boldly. He reached out to scare him and chase him away. The rooster tricked him and flew high up on the tree. The cat kept looking at the rooster and decided to wake up when it crows from the very next day.

Moral: Do not be proud of bad habits.

THE OXEN AND THE WHEELS

A pair of oxen was drawing a heavy load in a wagon along a country road. It was a long journey. The oxen used all their strength to drag the wagon, and they did not complain and worked hard. The wagon's wheels creaked at each turn and complained a lot. Then the wagon came into an area that had a lot of mud. The oxen pulled the wagon with all their might, but it was difficult as the mud was deep. The wheels complained loudly. This time the oxen lost their temper. "Silence wheels, we are drawing the wagon and not you.

We are quiet, and you must not complain as well." The wheels became calm, and the oxen were able to continue the journey.

Moral: They complain most who suffer the least.

THE LIONESS AND THE YOUNG JACKAL

Long ago, a lion couple lived in a thick forest with their two cubs. The couple was kind-hearted. One day, while searching for food, the lion found a baby jackal separated from his parents. He thought, "I should not make such a small creature my food", and took him home.

The lioness was very happy to see the baby jackal and decided to raise him with her cubs. Soon the baby jackal and lion cubs became friends, and they played together and grew up like siblings gradually.

One day, the young jackal and the young lions went deep into the forest. There they saw an elephant. The young jackal got frightened and stopped and said to the young lions, "Brothers, do not go near this huge creature. He will crush us under his feet," and ran away.

Reaching home, the lion cubs told the whole story to their mother. This made the jackal very angry. He shouted, “I am not a coward, come out, I will show you what I am.”

When the lioness heard these words, she intervened and said, “Dear, you are not inferior to any of the animals, but animals of your family do not prey on elephants. You are a jackal and not a lion. We have raised you like our own child. But, now that you talk of revenge, you must leave and live among your clan.”

Though surprised, the young jackal at once fled from the lion’s cave to find his clan.

Moral: Know the truth about yourself and act accordingly.

THE BIRDS AND THE MONKEYS

Once upon a time, there was a huge tree on the banks of a river. Some birds had built their nests on this tree and were living happily.

Once, it started raining very heavily. Some monkeys who were playing near the tree got drenched and ran for shelter under the tree.

When the birds saw the monkeys, they felt sorry for them. One of the birds addressing the monkeys said, "If you had built a home like us, you would not have to shiver like this."

Hearing this, the monkeys got annoyed. They climbed up the tree and destroyed the nests of the birds. The poor birds flew here and there, and they realised that advice should be given to learned, wise, and only to those who ask for it.

Moral: Never advise unless you are asked for it.

Tales from Panchatantra

Book-2

DREAMLAND PUBLICATIONS

J-128, Kirti Nagar, New Delhi -110 015, India

Tel : +91-11-2510 6050, 2543 5657

E-mail : dreamland@dreamlandpublications.com

Shop online at www.dreamlandpublications.com

Follow us on www.instagram.com/dreamland.publications

THE HYPOCRITE CAT

Long ago, there lived a partridge in a safe and warm hollow under a tree. One day, the partridge went out in search of food. While the partridge was away, a hare started living in its home. After some days, when the partridge returned home, he saw the hare comfortably living in his home. The partridge got annoyed and shouted, "How dare you live in my house?"

The hare replied, "It might have been yours, but now it's mine." A fight began between the hare and the partridge. Many animals and birds gathered and said to them, "Don't fight. Go find a judge for a solution to your problem."

This suggestion appealed to both of them, and they set out in search of a judge. After some time, they saw a cat sitting near the bank of a river. The cat was delighted to see the partridge and the hare coming and thought, "I will have a nice meal today." She looked at them and said, "What is the trouble with you, my children?"

"We need your help to settle a fight between us," said the hare. The cat said, "Children, I am not able to hear you properly. Please come closer."

The partridge and the hare sensed danger. They immediately fled from there, saving their lives, and decided not to fight anymore.

Moral: Bad people always take advantage of other people's fights.

ELEPHANTS AND THE KING MICE

Once, an earthquake ruined a village, and the villagers were forced to leave their houses and settle elsewhere. A group of mice began to live in the destroyed homes. There was a big lake next to the village. A herd of elephants used to visit the lake for drinking water. On their way to the lake, they used to crush hundreds of mice daily under their heavy feet. The King Mice went to the Elephant King and requested, "Sir, when your herd crosses the village, thousands of my subjects get crushed under the feet of your herd. Kindly change your route, and perhaps we can help you someday in return."

The King Elephant was kind-hearted. He smiled and said, "You mice are too small to be of any help to giants like us. But we will honour your request and change our path to the lake." After that, the group of mice lived happily until one day, while the mice were playing, they heard loud shouts of elephants coming from the direction of the lake.

The King Mice sensed that the elephants were in some danger. He asked some of the strong mice in his group to come along and went in the direction of that sound. Near the lake, they saw the elephants were caught in thick nets. The mice quickly nibbled the net, and soon the elephants were set free. The King Elephant thanked the mice and said, "I was wrong. I will never judge anyone again by their appearance."

Moral: At times, appearance is deceptive.

THE SNAKE AND THE FROGS

Once, there was an old snake. He was weak because of age and could not hunt anymore. He planned and went to a lake that had many frogs. He lay on the lakeside and did not try to eat the frogs. The frogs were surprised. "Why are you not attacking us," the frogs asked him from far. The snake said that a holy sage had ordered him to serve frogs and treat them as his master. The frogs were very happy to hear this. So, when the snake suggested that he can give the frogs rides on his back, they agreed. A week passed like this. One day, the tired snake said that he could not give them rides. The frogs said, "You must be hungry. You can eat one of us every day so that you have energy." The snake had planned this, and the frogs did not know they had fallen into the snake's trap. The snake now ate all the frogs one by one.

Moral: Do not get fooled by someone's sweet talk.

THE FOOLISH PERSON

Once, a fool wanted to sell his horse and goat. He tied a bell around the goat's neck and the end of its string to the horse's tail and went to the market. On the way, two crooks made a plan to cheat the fool and take the goat and the horse. One of them tied the bell to the horse's tail. The other crook went to the fool and told him that his horse had a bell tied to its tail. The fool was shocked and started to cry for his goat. "You should go and search for your goat," the crook suggested. The fool searched for his missing goat, and the other crook ran away with his horse. In this way, he lost both his horse and his goat.

Moral: Give up foolish ways.

THE BIRD WITH TWO HEADS

Once, there was a bird that was very strange as it had two heads. Each head of the bird had its own mind. The heads were friends, and the bird led a good life. But one day, the heads started fighting on a fruit they saw upon a tree. Both of them wanted the fruit, and there was only one fruit. The heads then decided that they would not fight on the fruit and instead tell the bird to eat it as they belonged to the bird only. In the fight, the minds in the heads did not look carefully at the fruit and did not bother to find out if it was healthy or poisonous. The fruit was a poisonous one. So, the minute the bird ate the fruit, it became seriously ill, leaving both the minds in the heads useless.

Moral: Having a conflicting state of mind is dangerous.

THE FOX AND THE GRAPES

Once, it was a hot day. A hungry fox wandered through the forest in search of food. He reached a vineyard at last, where there were many bunches of grapes. The fox decided to steal a bunch of grapes. He jumped high, but he could not reach them. The grapes were too high. The fox did not give up and repeatedly tried to get the grapes but failed each time. It started to get dark. The fox got tired and gave up. As he walked away, he looked at the grapes and said, "I'm sure the grapes were sour anyway."

Moral: Nothing comes easy without hard work. So, work hard and reach your goals.

THE HORSE AND THE LION

Long ago, there was a farmer who owned a horse. When the horse became old, the farmer asked the horse to leave his house and live elsewhere. Listening to his master's words, the horse became very sad. So the farmer said, "You can stay with me provided you bring me a lion's skin." Disheartened, the horse set out for the forest. There he met a fox and narrated his story. The fox decided to help the horse and advised, "You lie down here on the ground and pretend to be dead." The horse followed what the fox suggested. The clever fox at once went to the lion and said, "Your Majesty! A dead horse is lying in your kingdom. Come, we shall pull the horse and put it behind the trees so that you can enjoy a peaceful meal."

The lion believed the fox's words and followed him. On reaching the spot, the fox said, "Sir, if you permit, I will tie your tail to this dead horse." The lion agreed without having a question. The clever fox tied the lion's tail and the horse's tail together and asked the horse to run as fast as possible until he reached the farmer's house. All this happened so suddenly that the lion could not do anything. The horse ran very fast, dragging the lion over the stones, thorns, and bushes, injuring the lion. The horse stopped at his master's house with the unconscious lion tied to its tail. The farmer was surprised to see the lion and promised to take care of the horse all his life. The horse thanked the clever fox.

Moral: The mind is mightier than the body.

THE FAITHFUL DOG

Once, there lived an old rich man in a village. He had a dog named Mighty. Both of them loved each other. One night, when the old man was sleeping, Mighty saw a thief entering the house and started barking loudly, and the thief ran away. But this disturbed the old man. He looked around and asked, "Mighty, why are you barking? The next day, the same thief once again came. After filling his bag with the old man's riches, the thief left. This time, Mighty did not bark and quietly followed him. The thief dug a hole behind the house and buried the bag in it. The following day, the old man saw his treasure chest empty. He started to wail, but Mighty pulled his master's shirt and brought him to where the thief hid his valuables.

Within minutes Mighty dug out the bag and gave it to his master. The old man embraced Mighty and thanked him.

Moral: Faithfulness makes not only human beings but even animals great.

AN ANT AND A GRASSHOPPER

Once upon a time, there lived two friends, an ant and a grasshopper. The ant was a hard worker, whereas the grasshopper was a lazy fellow. One summer afternoon, while the grasshopper was playing his violin and enjoying the day, the ant was carrying a piece of cheese and taking it to his house with great effort.

On seeing his hardworking friend, the grasshopper laughed and said, "Why don't you come and play with me? The sun is hot, don't work so hard." "No," replied the ant. "After summer comes autumn, and after autumn comes winter. I must work, collect food and store it up for winters."

After a few weeks, autumn turned into winter, and the sun was hardly seen, and it became freezing cold.

The grasshopper was now shivering with cold and had trouble finding food. A day came when he had nothing to eat. He remembered his friend ant's words and realised he should not have wasted all his time singing and resting.

Moral: Work hard today, and you can reap the benefits tomorrow.

THE WOLF AND HIS SHADOW

There was a wolf that left his lair in the jungle, one evening. He was in a very good mood and wanted to find a prey to fulfil his appetite. He ran around here and there till the sun began to set.

As the wolf looked at his shadow, he was impressed with its large size. "I have grown in an impressive manner. I think I can fight the lion himself." Just then an even larger shadow covered his. He looked up. It was the lion. The wolf ran deep into the forest after looking at the lion and his shadow.

Moral: Do not forget realities.

THE FLIES AND THE HONEY-POT

Once, many flies were attracted to a jar of honey inside a hut. Their honeycomb was on the tree just outside the window. They smelled the honey and came inside the hut through the open window. The flies ate the honey, greedily. They got stuck to the pot of honey and could not fly away. Soon, they started to feel suffocated and stopped trying. They were tired of trying to take flight.

They exclaimed, "We are foolish. For honey, we took such a heavy risk. Our comb is full of honey. We did not need to come here at all."

Moral: Pleasure bought with pain, hurts.

THE TALE OF TWO CATS

Long ago, there lived two cats. One of them was fat, and the other was very thin. One day, the thin cat asked the fat cat, "You are so healthy and it seems your master feeds you very well."

The fat cat replied, "No, my dear! I go to the palace every night and hide under the King's table. There I feed on the delicious pieces of a variety of food that drop from the table." The thin cat, too, went to the palace with the fat cat that night.

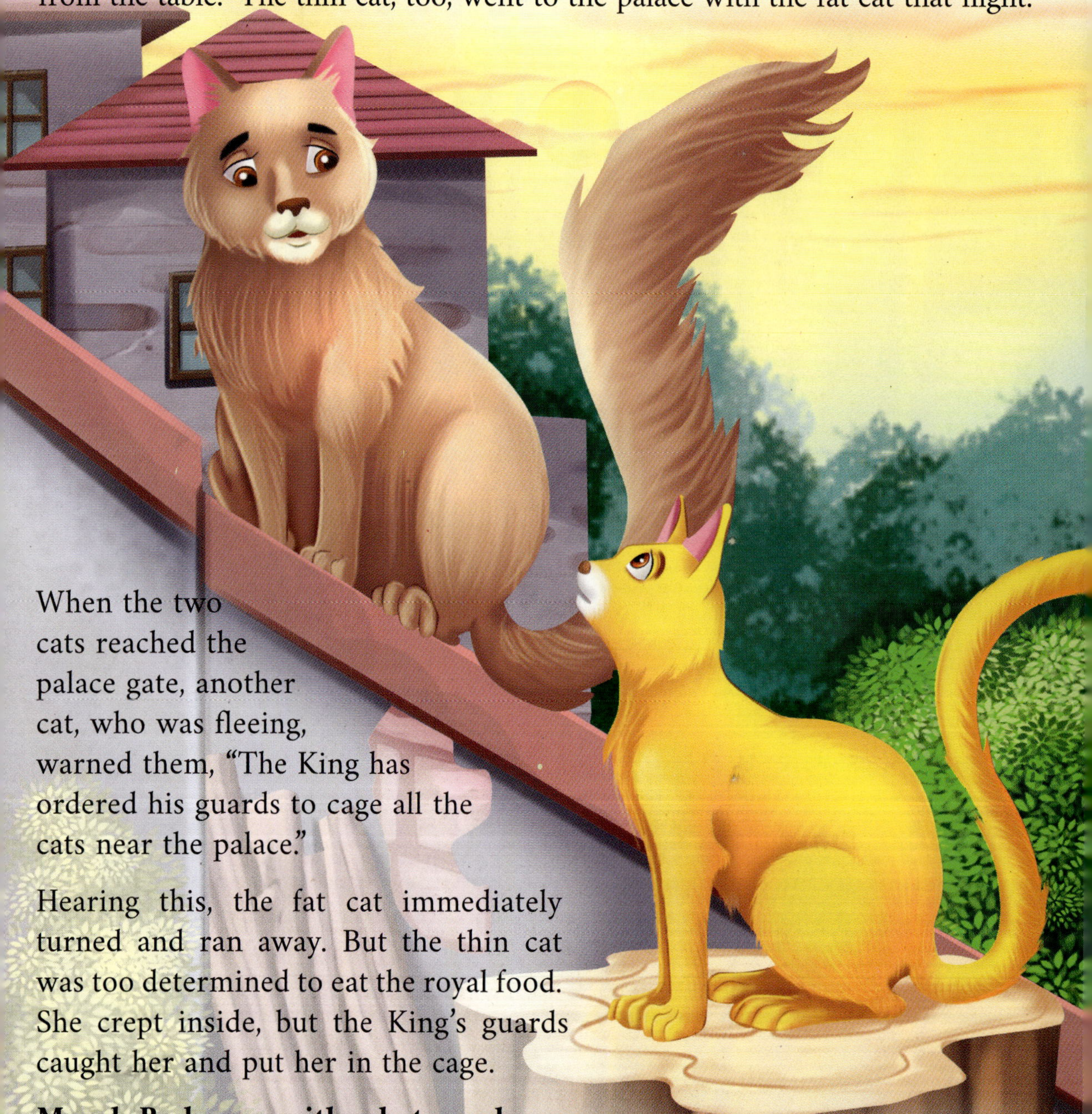

When the two cats reached the palace gate, another cat, who was fleeing, warned them, "The King has ordered his guards to cage all the cats near the palace."

Hearing this, the fat cat immediately turned and ran away. But the thin cat was too determined to eat the royal food. She crept inside, but the King's guards caught her and put her in the cage.

Moral: Be happy with what you have.

Tales from Panchatantra

Book-6

DREAMLAND PUBLICATIONS

J-128, Kirti Nagar, New Delhi -110 015, India

Tel : +91-11-2510 6050, 2543 5657

E-mail : dreamland@dreamlandpublications.com

Shop online at www.dreamlandpublications.com

Follow us on www.instagram.com/dreamland.publications

THE GOLDEN GOAT

It so happened that once there was a big goat that had golden fur. Its fur shone like fire, and all the animals feared it. One day the golden goat was hungry and went to eat vegetables in a garden. The vegetables were juicy and the goat ate many of them happily. The farmer saw the golden goat, ran to it with his stick, and threw him out of his garden. The lion sitting nearby saw this and said, "I have been so foolish to be scared of the goat due to its golden fur. Now I will not be scared anymore." The animals stopped feeling scared of the goat because of its golden fur.

Moral: Looks can be deceptive.

THE JACKAL AND THE DRUM

One day, a hungry jackal wandered far away from his home in search of food. He reached a deserted battlefield. Roaming about, he only found a drum there that the army had left behind. When the wind blew hard, the branches of a tree moved and hit the drum, making a loud noise. The jackal got scared listening to the noise and decided to run away from there. As he ran further away, he had second thoughts. He returned to explore the noise. He found the drum and realized that it was harmless. Under the drum, the jackal found some food. He was glad that he had returned after running away. The hungry jackal ate the food gladly.

Moral: Do not react blindly with fear.

THE STUBBORN HUNTER

Once upon a time, there lived a hunter in a village. He loved hunting rabbits. Many a time his friends advised him to give up hunting, but he did not pay any attention to them.

One day, one of his friends said, "I only wanted to warn you that killing innocent animals is a sin and all sinners get punished some day in their lives."

Just as the hunter was about to raise his knife, it slipped out of his hand and landed on his leg.

The hunter realised his mistake and from that day he gave up hunting and became a civilised man and lead a righteous life.

Moral: One must always be punished for doing bad deeds.

THE DONKEY AND THE GRASSHOPPER

Once, there was a donkey who worked for a farmer. One fine day, he heard grasshoppers chirping in the field. He loved their enchanting chirp a lot. He also wanted to chirp like the grasshoppers.

So, he went up to the grasshoppers and asked them what they ate and drank. The grasshoppers told him that they only took dew. The donkey also decided to take only dew like them to get a chirping voice.

He was happy with his plan. But only taking dew as food and drink, made the donkey thin and ill. All his friends got worried. The donkey decided to go back to his routine way of eating after a few days.

Moral: The law of nature is unchangeable.

THE BULL AND THE LITTLE MOUSE

On a hot summer day, a bull was sleeping under a tree. A mouse was passing that way, and he was looking at the bull. The bull was snoring loudly while sleeping. The mouse climbed up to the bull's nose and it playfully went into the bull's nostrils and bit the bull inside the nostril. The bull snorted so hard that the mouse fell out down. The bull woke up and shouted angrily and asked, "Who woke me up from my sleep?" The mouse replied, "Sorry! Mr. Bull, I was the one who just bit you for fun. I did not want to wake you up, Sir." Please forgive me for what I did.

The bull got angry and rushed forward to hit the small creature. The mouse ran very fast to save his life. At last, he found a stone wall that had a small hole. The bull came and reached up to the wall. He was not able to get hold of the mouse. He made a loud sound and said, "You silly creature! I will teach you a lesson, " and dashed against the wall. The wall was too strong for the bull. The bull hit the wall hard several times but could not break it.

The mouse said, "Why are you breaking your head for a small thing? Just leave it, Mr. Bull." Hearing this, the bull immediately left the place.

Moral: Might is not always right.

THE CROW AND THE QUAIL

Once there was a crow and quail who were friends. The crow was wicked, but the quail was innocent and simple. One day both the crow and the quail were very hungry.

They saw a milkman arriving with a pot of curd towards them. The crow happily said, "Look, our food is arriving." The quail warned the crow, but the crow said, "You don't worry, friend, just watch how I have the curd and be safe too." Just then, the milkman kept the pot of curd and rested for a while. The crow happily swooped down and had the curd to its heart's fill.

The quail said, "Now you had but do not go there again, or the milkman will catch you."

The milkman woke up and started walking towards the village to sell the curd. He could see that the quantity of curd was much lesser than before. He saw a crow and quail flying above him. The quail kept saying, don't have the curd from the milkman's pot, but the crow didn't listen.

The milkman could also see there was some curd in the beak of the crow. The milkman understood that why the quantity of curd had decreased. The milkman picked up a stone to hit the crow in a rage, but the crow flew high up away. The quail was not alert, and it got hit by the stone and was injured for no fault of its. We must never be in bad company, or we will have to face the effect on ourselves.

Moral: Your Company impacts your life.

THE LION AND THE HARE

It was a very hot day in the forest. The lion was very hungry. He came out of his den and went here and there to search for food. But he found no prey. Finally, he spotted a small hare.

Just then, a deer passed by. The lion became greedy. He thought; "Instead of this small hare, let me catch the deer. "

But the deer saw the lion and vanished into the forest. The lion returned to the hare but he had also run away. The lion had to return to his den, hungry.

Moral: A bird in the hand is worth two in the bush.

THE SHEPHERD AND THE SHEEP

Once, there was a shepherd. He had many sheep. He was bored of his work of tending sheep. He had to spend a lot of time taking them out for grazing and searching for the missing ones. So, he sold his sheep and bought many bags of dates. He decided to travel around the world on a ship and sell the dates. His brother accompanied him. On the way, a storm hit and their ship sank. With great difficulty, both managed to swim to an island. Soon, when the ocean was calm, they looked around and found many wild sheep. Being a shepherd, they were able to train them to become domestic sheep. After some days, another ship came sailing by and the shepherd and his brother were rescued. They took the sheep with them. They pledged to always care for the sheep and not change their profession.

Moral: Be happy with what you have.

THE CAT AND THE KITTENS

There was an actor who kept a cat in his house. The cat also had four playful kittens that were always roaming the house. One day, the kittens found a mask that belonged to the actor. One of the kittens wore the mask and started showing off before the other kittens. The other kittens told her that she looked very good with the mask. The kitten kept the mask on her face and went to show it to her mother. The mother cat told her to go and keep the mask where she had found it and not pick things that belonged to the actor and others. The kitten realised her fault and did as she had been told. Then it went to play with the other kittens.

Moral: Never touch things of others without their permission.

THE LARK AND THE WHEAT FIELD

Once, a lark made a nest in a wheat field. Her eggs hatched and slowly her young ones grew. One day, the young ones said, "Mother we should move out from here.

We heard the farmer say that the wheat is ripe and he is going to call his friends and relatives to harvest the crop."

The mother lark said to her young ones, "No, there will be no harvesting as he is depending on his relatives and friends. We can stay."

The next day, the young ones said to mother lark, "Mother, let us go, the farmer came to the field with his sons. Tomorrow, they will start their harvesting," The mother lark replied, "It is time to move now as the farmer will harvest the wheat himself with his sons." The lark and its young ones flew away.

Moral: Self-help is the best help.

THE DEER AND THE HUNTER

A deer was drinking water from a pool. He admired himself in the reflection and said, "I have such strong horns with beautiful antlers! But I am sad because my legs are ugly and not worthy of my beautiful face and horns." He made a long face.

Just then, a hunter approached and shot an arrow at the deer. The deer darted and ran for safety. As he ran fast, he had to pass through a few low trees. Running past them, his antlers got stuck in them. The hunter was still chasing the deer.

He moved his legs harder and unstuck himself. Then he ran away to safety. The hunter could not take away the deer. The deer considered his legs useless but they saved him from danger.

Moral: We often despise what is most useful to us.

THE HARE AND HIS FRIENDS

Once, a hare heard the hounds running towards him and getting closer. The hare went to the horse and said, “Please can you save me from the hounds?” The horse replied, “I am really busy with my work right now and cannot help you.” The hare was disappointed but he went to the bull to request him to scare the hounds away. The bull said, “I am not free. I have to go to the field for ploughing.”

The goat and the ram also refused to help the hare. The hounds had come very close by now. No other friends were willing to help the hare. By this time the hare saw that the hounds were quite near. The hare ran away fast and escaped.

Moral: One who has too many friends, has no real friend.

THE SWALLOW AND THE OTHER BIRDS

Many years ago, a farmer sowed hemp seeds in his field. A swallow and some other birds were hopping there. "Beware of the farmer," said the swallow to all the other birds."Why?" Asked the other birds. They did not understand why the swallow was warning them. "That is hemp seed that the farmer is sowing; be careful" warned the swallow.

After some time the hemp grew into full plants. The farmer made the hemp into a cord. From the cord, the farmer made a strong net. He used the net to catch all the birds.

The swallow was sad to see the captured birds and said, "I wish they had heeded my warning and picked up all the hemp seeds." He flew away to another land.

Moral: Destroy the seed of evil, or it will grow up to your ruin.

Tales from Panchatantra

Book-3

DREAMLAND PUBLICATIONS

J-128, Kirti Nagar, New Delhi -110 015, India

Tel : +91-11-2510 6050, 2543 5657

E-mail : dreamland@dreamlandpublications.com

Shop online at www.dreamlandpublications.com

Follow us on www.instagram.com/dreamland.publications

THE SPARROWS AND THE ELEPHANT

Long ago, a sparrow couple lived in a comfortable nest on a branch of a huge banyan tree in a jungle. The female sparrow laid eggs and the couple was delighted.

One day, a mighty elephant came wandering near the tree. He was very proud of his strength. The elephant started to pull down a branch of the tree with his huge trunk. The sparrow couple saw him and pleaded, "Dear brother, our nest is built on this tree and there are eggs inside the nest. Please don't pull this branch." But the arrogant elephant did not pay any attention to the sparrow couple and pulled out a big branch. The eggs fell from the nest and broke.

The female sparrow cried bitterly, and the friends of the sparrow couple, the crow couple, the frog, and the flies came to find out what had happened. They sat together to plan and teach the elephant a lesson.

The next day, when the elephant was going to the lake, the flies flew near his ears to make a buzzing sound to irritate the elephant and he closed his eyes. The crow couple immediately swooped down and pecked both eyes of the elephant. The elephant was baffled by these sudden attacks.

Finally, the frog began croaking aloud. The elephant thought he was close to the lake. The very next moment, he fell inside a deep ditch and learnt a lesson for his arrogance.

Moral: Intelligence wins over might.

THE MOSQUITO AND THE LION

Once, a mosquito went to a lion and arrogantly said, “I am not afraid of you. I am stronger than you. You have sharp claws and teeth to attack. Let us fight so we can decide who is stronger.” The mosquito said this and to prove himself, he bit the lion’s nose. The lion felt the sting and tried to catch the mosquito in his claws to crush it. But instead, he scratched his nose, and it started to bleed. The mosquito was thrilled and buzzed off, elated in victory. He was so happy that he did not see where he was flitting and got entangled in a spider’s web. The spider caught him!

Moral: Pride over success should not throw us off our guard.

THE BEAR AND THE BEES

Once a bear was wandering in search of food. He passed by a log where a swarm of bees had made their honeycomb. As the bear tried to sniff it, a bee stung him sharply.

This action of the bee made the bear lose his temper. He swatted at the honeycomb with his paws. But this enraged the entire swarm of bees and they attacked him all over. The poor bear had to run to save himself.

Moral: Misdeeds bring in trouble.

THE FROG AND THE FOX

There was a frog that lived in the pond in the marshes. He decided to become a doctor. He came out of the pond and went and sat on a big rock.

There he loudly croaked to proclaim, "I am a learned doctor. I can give the right medicines to cure diseases." The animals of the forest were impressed and started to go to the frog to avail his services.

One day, a fox called out, "You a doctor! How can you set up to heal others when you cannot even cure your own lame legs. Look at your blotched and wrinkled skin! Can you cure it?"

The frog did not know what to say. He felt ashamed when all the animals started to laugh. He went back to the pond.

Moral: First, heal thyself.

THE LION AND THE HUMBLE MAN

Once, there was a man who lost his way in the forest.

There he came across a lion that had a thorn in his paw. The lion was in pain.

The man was kind-hearted. He went close to the lion and removed the thorn. The lion licked the man's hand and went away. After some days the man went to a zoo and accidentally fell into a lion's cage.

The lion came and sat at the feet of the man.

The man realized that it was the same lion that he had met in the forest. The lion had remembered the man and helped him showing his gratitude.

Moral: We get the rewards for our helpful acts in return.

THE MONKEYS AND A BELL

Once, the forest monkeys found a bell, and they started to play with it and made a terrible noise.

The villagers thought, "There must be a monster in the forest. He is ringing the bell." The villagers got very scared, and they decided to leave the kingdom.

One brave lady saw the monkeys playing with the bell. She went to the king and said, "Your Majesty! The monster can be conquered. But I need payment if I do the work." The king agreed to pay her a large sum of money.

The woman collected a lot of fruits. She pretended to pray. Later, she kept those fruits under a tree in the forest. When the monkeys saw the fruits, they dropped the bell. The monkeys got busy eating the fruits. The clever woman picked up the bell and ran back to the kingdom. She got rewarded for her intelligence.

Moral: Intelligence and courage will bring success.

THE ANT AND THE FLY

Once, an ant and fly began to fight on who is more important. The fly said to the ant, "Ant, you might work hard all day but I am more important than you. I pass my time with the rich and famous. I do not have to work and can just spend my time eating delicious food at the temple."

The ant replied, "You should not be proud. Everyone is irritated when you are at the temple. You do not have any food in winter as you do not collect food like me in summer. When you shiver in the cold, I am safe and at peace in my comfortable home. I am prepared to live in any season of the year."

The fly was ashamed and flew away.

Moral: Without labour, nothing prospers.

THE DONKEY, THE FOX, AND THE LION

One day a donkey and a fox became friends and promised that they would help each other in times of need. After some days, they went into the forest for hunting, where they met a lion who wanted to catch them.

The fox had a sly idea and went and told the lion that he would help him catch the donkey if he would let him go free. The lion agreed. The fox went to the donkey and led him to a deep pit. The donkey fell into the pit. The fox went to tell the lion. The lion went to the pit to catch the donkey, but the donkey had nimble feet, and he had hopped out and run away. The lion chased away the fox.

Moral: Betray a friend, and you will often find you have ruined yourself.

THE DEER AND THE VINE

Once, two hunters were in the forest. They saw a deer. They started chasing it to catch it. The deer darted away fast to save his life. He saw a thick vine and hid behind its thick and large leaves.

The hunters went past the vine as the deer was well hidden behind it. After some time, the deer was sure that he was safe. He was hungry. He started to nibble at the leaves of the vine. Just then the hunters returned and spotted the deer behind the eaten leaves.

The hunters easily captured the deer from near the vine in their net. The deer regretted eating the vine leaves.

Moral: Do not harm your saviour.

THE ELEPHANT AND THE TAILOR

Once there lived a tailor in a village who had his shop near a river. An elephant also lived in the same village and they both were good friends.

Every day the elephant used to go to the river to take bath. On the way, he always stopped at the tailor's shop and the tailor used to give him a banana.

One day, the tailor had a quarrel with a customer and hence he was upset. When the elephant came and put his trunk for his daily banana, the tailor pricked his trunk with a needle.

The elephant was hurt. He went back to the river and filled his trunk with muddy water. Then he rushed towards the tailor's shop and sprayed the muddy water on some new dresses the tailor had made. The tailor understood his mistake and apologised to the elephant for his misdeed.

Moral: Never misbehave with anyone.

THE THIRSTY CROW

It was a hot summer day. A crow was very thirsty and searched for water everywhere but could not find any.

He saw a pot in the garden which had some water in it. The water was so low that the crow could not drink it.

The crow's eyes fell on a pile of pebbles lying nearby. The crow picked up the pebbles and dropped them into the pot. As more pebbles filled the pot, the water level in the pot came up high. The crow drank the water happily to quench his thirst and flew away.

Moral: If you work hard, you will find an answer to your problem.

THE GOLDEN BIRD AND THE KING

Long ago, there lived a golden bird that laid golden eggs. One day, a young hunter saw this strange bird and caught it. On the way, the hunter started dreaming that the golden bird would lay golden eggs and soon he would be rich. Another thought cropped up in his mind. "It could be dangerous to keep the bird because if the king comes to know about my richness, he might think I am a thief. The hunter went to the palace and gifted the bird to the king, and he said, "Your Majesty, this is not an ordinary bird. This is a magical bird which lays golden eggs."

The king was pleased with the gift, but one guard created doubt and said, "O' king, this hunter is fooling you. If this bird lays golden eggs, then why did he present it to you?"

The king ordered his guards to release the birds in the forest. The bird flew back to its nest and thought, "This seems to be a kingdom of fools. The hunter knew that I laid golden eggs, yet he gifted me to the king. The king's guards doubted my magical powers, and I was set free."

Moral: One should make a decision only after checking the facts.

A CUNNING FRIEND

Once there lived a camel and a jackal near a river. They were good friends. Every day, they used to go to the river to drink water. There was a sugarcane field on the other side of the river. One day, both the friends decided to enjoy the juicy sugarcanes.

The camel carried his friend on his back, and they ate a lot of sugarcanes. After some time, the jackal started howling in a loud voice. The camel asked him not to do so, but the jackal didn't listen, saying it was their habit.

His howling attracted the attention of the farmers, and they came there. The jackal being small, jumped away, but the camel was badly beaten.

The camel somehow escaped and reached the river bank. To teach a lesson, while going back the camel began to roll in the water. The jackal told him not to do so, but the camel said, "We camels have a habit of doing this after meals."

The jackal had now learned his lesson and repented his mistake.

Moral: As you sow, so shall you reap.

Tales from Panchatantra

Book-4

DREAMLAND PUBLICATIONS
J-128, Kirti Nagar, New Delhi -110 015, India
Tel : +91-11-2510 6050, 2543 5657
E-mail : dreamland@dreamlandpublications.com
Shop online at www.dreamlandpublications.com
Follow us on www.instagram.com/dreamland.publications

THE BUG AND THE FLEA

A white flea lived between the soft bedsheets of a king's bed. It fed on the king's blood and was very happy in life. One day, a bug came by. He said that he wanted to taste the king's blood. The flea was uncomfortable as a bug's sting is painful and the king would know if he stung him to taste blood.

On the bug's insistence, the flea agreed. "But you have to wait till the king falls asleep." The bug agreed but couldn't control itself and it bit the king as soon as he lied on the bed to sleep. The king was furious, and he told his guards to check his bed for bugs. The bug and the flea quickly hid. The flea told the bug to leave the palace at once.

Moral: Do not trust the words of strangers, for they could be false promises.

THE HARES AND THE FROGS

Once, there was a group of hares. They lived together. They were troubled because of the hunters who came to hunt them. All the hares were scared for their lives.

The leader of the hares was fed up with living such a frightening life. He told the hares, "We are always scared. We should not be scared and change our attitude." All the hares nodded their heads in agreement.

When they went to the lake, where many frogs lived, they were surprised to find them scared. The frogs saw the hares and jumped into the lake to hide themselves. The leader said, "Look at the frogs, they are frightened of us. We also fear the hunters like this. Let us not be scared anymore and lead our lives confidently."

Moral: Keep a positive attitude.

THE DONKEY AND THE SALT

Once, there was a salt seller. He went with his donkey to the market every day. He carried a salt bag on his donkey's back. One day, when they were on the way to the market, they crossed a stream. The donkey tumbled into the stream, and his bag of salt fell into the water. The salt dissolved in the water. So, when the salt seller picked the salt bag and put it on the donkey's back, the bag was very light. The donkey was happy. He started to stumble and fall into the stream every day. The salt seller understood the donkey's trick. He decided to teach him a lesson. The next day, he loaded a bag of cotton on the donkey's back. When the donkey played the same trick, the water dampened the cotton. The bag was now heavy. The donkey had to carry a heavy load. He did not play the trick again on the salt seller.

Moral: Luck won't favour always.

THE MOUSE AND THE FROG

Once, there lived a mouse and a frog in the same area. Every morning, the frog would hop out of the pond and go to visit the mouse. The frog and the mouse would chat, and then the frog would return to the pond. One day, the frog got upset when he realised that the mouse had never visited him. He decided to force the mouse to come to his home. So, when he went to the mouse on his daily visit, he cleverly tied a string to the mouse's tail and the other end of the string to his own leg and hopped away. The mouse started getting dragged with the frog. The frog reached the pond and jumped in. However, the mouse did not know how to swim and started to drown. When the frog saw this, he quickly saved the mouse by bringing him back to land. The frog now apologised to the mouse.

Moral: Do not force friendship.

TWO FISHES AND A FROG

In a lake, there lived many fishes and a frog. The frog was a good friend of the two fish, and they spent a lot of time daily discussing the matters of the lake. However, one day, they overheard two fishermen planning to come fishing the next day to the lake. The frog immediately suggested to the fish that they must find another safe spot. But the fish were arrogant and did not agree to leave the lake. They were sure that they could scare the fishermen with their noisy movements in the water. The frog fled for his life and left the lake. After the frog left, the fishermen came the next day and caught a lot of fish, including the two fish, in their net.

Moral: Don't be overconfident in the face of danger. Think of safety first.

THE KING AND THE PARROTS

Once upon a time, a tribal king caught two parrots in his net. He started back on his journey home when one of the parrots escaped the trap and flew away. It flew to a sage's hut and started to live there. The other parrot lived with the tribal king. A few months passed. A king passed through the forest, and as he rode his horse, he came near the tribal king's house. He heard the parrot say, "Catch this man and beat him black and blue." The king decided to ride in the other direction. Soon, he reached the sage's hut. When the king came closer to the hut, the sage's parrot said politely, "You are welcome, sir. It is a pleasure to see you."The king was amazed.

Moral: A good environment and training always give better results. A person is known by the company he keeps.

THE CLEVER FOX AND THE CROW

Once, a crow got a piece of bread in its beak and was sitting on a tree to eat it. A fox saw this and started planning to take away that bread from the crow. The fox went close to the crow and started praising it and said, "I have heard that you sing very well. Many birds and animals have been praising your sweet voice, and I too wanted to hear some melodic tones from you." The crow could not understand the cleverness of the cunning fox. As soon as it opened its beak to sing, the piece of bread fell. The clever fox was waiting for this, picked up the bread, and ran away into the forest. The foolish crow just repented for its foolishness.

Moral: Do not believe in any evil beings' flattery.

THE MONGOOSE AND THE FARMER'S WIFE

Once there lived a farmer and his wife with their son in a small village. To protect their child, they brought a mongoose. One day, the farmer couple had to leave the house, leaving the child at home. Before leaving the house, the farmer's wife said to the mongoose, "The baby is sleeping. Take care of him. Don't leave him alone."

The farmer's wife returned home earlier and saw the mongoose sitting near the door with his mouth stained with blood. Without finding out the truth, she assumed that the mongoose had hurt her son. She picked up a big stone and hit the little mongoose, which made him run away from the house.

She found her son sleeping quietly and an injured cobra lying on the floor when she entered the house. She understood that the mongoose had saved her child. She repented for her mistake, but it was too late.

Moral: Do not do anything in haste.

THE FARMER'S WIFE AND THE CROW

A farmer grew many vegetables on a farm in his village. One day, he gave all the vegetables to his wife to sell them in the market. The wife carried the vegetables to the market. With the money earned, she bought some eggs.

The farmer's wife was excited and walked back home with the basket of eggs. She also had money in her purse. She was careless and was in a hurry.

Suddenly, she stumbled on the way and the eggs fell out of the basket and broke. The farmer's wife looked up at the crow on the tree and said, "You foolish crow. You cawed unpleasantly and I got distracted. Now all my eggs have broken." The crow said, "You were in a hurry, so you were not careful and I did not even caw!"

Moral: You should not blame others for your fault.

THE WICKED HERON

Once, a wicked heron lived near a pond. The heron once spoke to the fish with a worried look on his face, "Soon, the pond is going to dry up, and it will have only mud all around.

The fish, crab and the frogs became worried and asked the heron to give some idea. The heron was waiting for this opportunity and said, "There is a pond nearby which is full of water, and I can take you all there one by one." They all agreed, and the heron carried one of them daily and killed them for its meals. One day the crab said, "Why do you carry only fish and not the crabs to the other pond." The heron was happy to hear this and carried the crab. After flying for some distance, the crab saw fish bones on a rock and understood the heron's fatal plans. It immediately strangled the heron with its claws and saved its own life. The crab came back to the pond and narrated what happened; all the others heaved a sigh of relief and lived peacefully.

Moral: A timely wise act can save many lives.

THE TWO LIZARDS

On a warm winter morning, there were two lizards sitting on a wall on an old windmill. They were basking in the sunshine. One lizard was sad. The other one was wise and heard the sad lizard say, "No one notices us. We are lizards. Our life is so boring. I wish I was a deer with big strong horns."

Just then they saw a pack of hounds chase a deer that had big horns. The wise lizard said, "Did you see that? You are beautiful as you are. You are small and safe from danger." The sad lizard sighed with relief and said, "I am going to be happy as a lizard. I do not want to be a beautiful deer at all."

Moral: Never wish the unthinkable.

THE OWL AND THE NIGHTINGALE

Once, there was an owl. He lived in a temple that had a large library. There were all types of ancient books there. The owl studied these books. With time, he grew proud of his knowledge. "I am surely the most intelligent creature," he said to himself.

One day, the owl was sitting on a tree, outside the temple. He was quite sleepy. A nightingale came there and sat on the tree. She began to sing. The owl asked the bird who she was and asked her to be quiet saying that he is thinking wise things in his sleep.

The nightingale replied, "You must be foolish still after reading so many books. All know that I sing the sweetest songs but you do not know." The owl was embarrassed.

Moral: Do not pretend to be something you are not.

THE FLY AND THE MULE

One day, a mule was dragging a chariot. He was tired. While he was walking, a fly came and sat on the wheel of the vehicle. She said to the Mule, "Oh Mule, why are you walking so slowly? You look like a strong and big beast. You can surely walk faster." The mule was very angry. He turned to the fly and said, "I do not pay attention to what you say regarding me."

He said, "I only care about the person who rides the cart. He is my guide. If I walk slowly, he increases my speed. Therefore, you go away. I don't want to talk to someone who is so small and rude to me. I know when I have to walk fast and at what time I should walk slowly!"

Moral: Never give unnecessary advice.

THE APE AND THE BEE

Once, there was a big ape that lived in the forest. One day, he saw a thick golden syrup falling from a tree branch. "Yummy, that must be delicious honey," the ape declared. He looked up and saw a beehive and many bees buzzing around it.

The ape grew excited about climbing the tree and tasting the honey but he did not move. He remembered, "Last week, the bees had stung me. I suffered a lot. I will not do this again. I will come at dusk and steal honey from their beehive."

Just then a bee flew by. The ape spoke to the bee, "How are you able to make sweet honey, and at the same time, carry such a horribly painful sting?" The bee wisely said, "Our good work tastes sweet; but when someone tries to steal it, our anger is bitter! You can ask us for honey and we will surely give you some."

Moral: Better to ask than steal.

THE CROWS AND THE BAGS

Once, it was a rainy day, and two crows were lazy. The crows challenged each other to see which of them could fly highest while carrying a sack of the same size.

The first crow filled his sack with cotton and laughed at the other crow that had filled his sack with salt.

It began to rain, as the second crow had expected, the salt started to dissolve. The cotton absorbed the rainwater and became so heavy that the first crow did not even have the strength to let it off the ground, and he had to admit defeat.

Moral: One must foresee the consequences and take action.

'Tales from Panchatantra' is a set of 10 books having kids' all-time favourite stories with effective moral lessons. These stories retold in a simple language and illustrated in the most suitable way will teach the basic skills of life to children. These stories are the best way to instil moral life values and entertain the budding little readers as well.

DREAMLAND PUBLICATIONS
J-128, Kirti Nagar, New Delhi -110 015, India
Tel. : +91-11-2510 6050, 2543 5657
E-mail : dreamland@dreamlandpublications.com
Shop online at www.dreamlandpublications.com
Follow us www.instagram.com/dreamland.publications

SCAN ME

Tales from Panchatantra
Book-5

Tales from Panchatantra

Book-5

DREAMLAND PUBLICATIONS

J-128, Kirti Nagar, New Delhi -110 015, India

Tel : +91-11-2510 6050, 2543 5657

E-mail : dreamland@dreamlandpublications.com

Shop online at www.dreamlandpublications.com

Follow us on www.instagram.com/dreamland.publications

THE TORTOISE AND THE EAGLE

A tortoise was basking in the sun. He was complaining to the sea birds, "My fate is so bad, no one is teaching me how to fly." An eagle was flying by and asked about the matter. The tortoise said that he wanted to learn to fly.

The eagle asked for a reward and agreed to teach the tortoise to fly.

The eagle picked the tortoise with his claws and took him up in the sky. He let him go and called out, "Fly." The tortoise crashed on the ground with a thud.

The tortoise felt sorry said, "I have accepted my present fate now. Thank God for blessing me with a shell that saved my life."

Moral: If men had all they wished, they would be often ruined.

THE LION AND THE ELEPHANT

One day, the lion sat near a rock. He was a strong animal, yet each time he heard the rooster crow, he got scared. The lion thought, "I am the strongest and bravest, and I am the king of the jungle. But a rooster scares me with just cawing. Just then, an elephant came there and asked the lion what troubled him.

The lion asked him, "Can anything harm a beast like you who has tremendous bulk and strength?" The elephant replied, "Do you see this little mosquito? If it stings me in the ear, I suffer bad pain."

The lion understood that even the strongest creatures have weak points, and he gained self-confidence.

Moral: We all have weak points. sInstead of complaining about them, we should focus on the pleasant things in life.

THE MONKEY AND THE CROCODILE

Long ago, there lived a monkey on a Jambolan tree by the side of the river. There also lived a crocodile in the river. Both of them became friends, and the monkey used to give tasty Jambolans to the crocodile. The crocodile once gave those fruits to his wife and she was thrilled to eat the tasty Jambolans. The crocodile's wife was a wicked woman. She said, "O dear, the monkey who eats these fruits every day would be even tastier to eat. Please bring this monkey's heart to me."

Although sad, the crocodile said to the monkey, “Dear friend, my wife has invited you home for dinner, please sit on my back, and I will take you home. When they reached the middle of the river, the crocodile said, “Dear friend, you know, my wife is unwell, and she can be cured only by eating a monkey’s heart.”

The clever monkey immediately said, “Oh my dear friend, you could have told me earlier. I would have been pleased to help your wife, but I left my heart on the tree. We should go back and get it.” The foolish crocodile believed the monkey, and they rushed back. As soon as they reached the tree, the monkey climbed up the tree and said, “Go away, you unfaithful friend. Can anyone take their heart and be alive?” The crocodile felt ashamed for his actions and went away.

Moral: Use intelligence to win in difficult situations.

THE CLEVER HARE

Once upon a time, a lion lived in the forest; he was very wicked and fierce. Once all the animals decided to talk to him. They said to him, "Sir, if you kill the animals like this, very soon the forest will be empty. So, we have decided to send one animal daily to your den as your food." The lion agreed happily.

From that day onwards, one animal was sent daily to the lion to become his food. One day it was the hare's turn and it reached the lion's den very late. The lion was hungry and impatient. He roared loud and asked, "Why are you so late?" The hare replied, "When I was coming to you, another lion stopped me on the way." The lion asked, "Another lion? How is it possible?"

"There cannot be another lion in this forest." The lion said. The hare took him to a nearby well and asked him to look inside. The lion saw his reflection and thinking it to be another lion, roared and asked, "Who are you?" The lion could hear his loud roar back as an echo but assumed that the other lion was challenging.

The lion became angry with rage and jumped into the well to fight the other lion. Not knowing how to swim, the lion was soon drowned. After learning everything, all animals praised the hare for his intelligence and lived happily after that.

Moral: Intelligence is superior to physical strength.

THE CHEETAH AND THE FOX

Once, there lived a cheetah and a fox in a forest. They were very good friends. They always hunted together and passed their time talking and chatting with each other.

One day, as they were walking near the river, the cheetah saw its reflection in the water and said, "I am so handsome. Look at my spots. They are bright black and so lovely."

The fox also said that its tail was bushy and it had a shiny coat too.

The cheetah and the fox continued the argument on who was more handsome. The fox knew that he was not really as handsome as the cheetah. So, finally, he said, "I know you are handsome but it would have been wonderful if you had brains like me."

The cheetah apologised for being vain. They continued to be good friends.

Moral: Never be vain.

THE DOG AND THE NEW LAND

A country was hit by famine badly. In that country, there lived a dog. He decided to go in search of food to a new country. He walked a long distance and reached another country. There he went here and there to find food. Finally, he reached a house with an open door. He went inside and ate to his heart's content. As he was leaving the house, some dogs chased him and bit him all over. The dog thought, "I think it is better to return to my land and live there in peace with what I have there than to get bitten." So, the dog returned home. When his friends and relatives came to meet him, they asked, "How was the new land you went to?" The dog replied, "There is plenty to eat in the new land. But the members of our own family try to harm us there."

Moral: The grass looks greener on the other side.

THE FOOLISH MONKEYS

A long time ago, in wintertime, a group of monkeys was feeling very cold. They talked to each other and decided to go to a village near their forest to sit by the warm fire. When the monkeys reached there and sat by the fire the villagers were angry. The villagers chased them away as they did not want monkeys in their village. The monkeys returned to the forest and decided that they would make their fire like the villagers. The monkeys collected wood and put red berries on it. They thought the red berries were coal and would make the fire. But there was no fire, and they were puzzled. The birds on the tree had a hearty laugh at the foolish monkeys. The monkeys were ashamed of their foolishness.

Moral: Gather complete knowledge of everything.

THE MARRIAGE OF THE SNAKE

There once lived a sage and his wife. They had no children. They prayed to God who blessed them with a snake child. The snake grew up.

The sage couple tried a lot but could not find a suitable girl for their young snake son. Finally, the sage was approached by a friend. "Oh! I'm looking for a match for my daughter. I shall give her in marriage to your snake son."

After marriage, the newly married couple-the girl and the snake started to live together. One night, the snake crawled out of the basket. After some time, a young man woke up the girl. He said to her, "I'm your husband."

When the sage and his wife came to know this, they quickly burnt the snake's skin. Their son was freed from the curse.

Moral: Presence of mind works in many situations.

THE TALKING CAVE

Once upon a time, a pair of jackals lived in the forest along with their cubs. Once there was a heavy storm in the forest. The mother jackal said, "Let's live in the lion's den." The father jackal asked, "Are you out of your mind? You mean we should go into the jaws of death ourselves?"

After a long wait and search, they found a lion's empty den and settled there. The father jackal was supposed to hide in the den and the mother jackal was to sit outside and guard the den. There was a fox very near to the jackal family who had heard the entire plan.

When the lion returned, the mother jackal made a loud noise and indicated to the father jackal about the lion's coming. The father jackal began beating the baby jackals to make them cry out loudly. The father jackal said, "Our children are crying for lion's meat." The mother jackal replied and said, "Don't worry. I can see a lion approaching and will get its meat soon." Hearing this, the lion panicked and fled away.

Seeing the lion fleeing, the fox laughed out loud and said that he can help the lion drive those animals out of his den. The lion agreed and said, “We will go there but you must tie your tail to mine.” The fox agreed to this and they went to the den together.

As they reached the den, the mother jackal said, “What is this you silly fox? I asked you to get me five lions and you are just bringing one? Then I will have to cook your meat too for my children.” Both the lion and the fox got scared and ran to save their lives. The jackal family lived happily thereafter in the lion’s den.

Moral: Intelligence can help us escape all the problems.

THE LAZY ELEPHANT

Once, there was a very lazy elephant that lived in the green forest. He walked around the forest and destroyed trees on the way. Small animals ran away in his fear. Plants and grass got trampled under his heavy feet. One day a fox spoke to the elephant, "Elephant, you are such a large animal. All the animals want you to be the king." The elephant was very glad to hear this and when he saw that even the other animals had already collected to talk to the elephant. The elephant promised not to trouble anyone from that day.

Moral: Mend your ways and take appreciation.

THE CAT AND THE RAT

Once four animals, the owl, rat, cat, and mongoose lived in the forest. One day, the cat got trapped in the hunter's net.

The rat went near the cat in the net and teased him. When the owl and the mongoose saw the rat freely jumping around, they wanted to catch him. The rat got scared and to save his life asked the cat if he could enter the net. He told the cat, "I promise to save you by cutting the net with my sharp teeth if you will help me. The cat was willing and allowed the rat to share the net with him. The rat cut the net and the cat was set free. The next day, the cat went to the rat's hole to offer friendship. However, the rat did not come out of his hole.

Moral: We should select our friends carefully.

THE BEAR AND TWO FRIENDS

Once there were two friends. They decided to go on a holiday. They had to cross a forest to reach their holiday spot. As they walked through the forest, a bear saw them. The bear came closer to them. The two friends got scared. One friend quickly climbed a tree. The other friend could not climb the tree. He lay on the ground and held his breath. The bear came to him and sniffed him. The bear thought the friend was dead. The bear went away. The friend on the tree came down and asked, "What did the bear whisper into your ears?" The friend replied, still sitting on the ground. "The bear asked me to keep away from friends like you."

Moral: A friend in need is a friend indeed.

Tales from Panchatantra

Book-7

DREAMLAND PUBLICATIONS

J-128, Kirti Nagar, New Delhi -110 015, India

Tel : +91-11-2510 6050, 2543 5657

E-mail : dreamland@dreamlandpublications.com

Shop online at www.dreamlandpublications.com

Follow us on www.instagram.com/dreamland.publications

THE CLEVER MONKEY CHIEF

Long ago, a troop of monkeys resided on a hill near a river.

On the riverbank, there was a mango tree full of fruits. The king of the land went fishing in the river one day. His workers discovered not only fish but also a few juicy mangoes as they pulled in the nets.

They took the mangoes to the king. The king took a bite of the juicy fruit and declared it to be wonderful. He made the decision to remove all the mangoes off the tree.

The king and his troops gathered many rafts and paddled up the river till they reached the mango tree's location. "Let us stay here tonight and collect the mangoes in the morning," the king told his men.

So the king and his warriors ate their meals and retired to their beds.

The monkeys feared death when they saw the king's warriors with their arrows drawn and fled to their Chief. "Dear Chief! "The king's troops are around the tree, waiting to shoot us," everyone said.

"Do not be scared! I'll come to your rescue. "Stay where you are until I call you," the Chief ordered.

The Monkey Chief then caught hold of a mango tree branch that hung over the river. "I'm going to build a bridge out of my back," he told himself.

As a result, the Monkey Chief reached across the river and grabbed the tree's longest branch. Run along the branch of the other tree, step on my back, and then run out on the other branch." The monkeys followed their Chief.

When all of the monkeys got safely across, the Monkey Chief fainted and lay motionless due to the stomping on his back. The king was so moved that he commanded his warriors to save the Monkey Chief and to never again hurt the monkeys.

Moral: Kindness always gets a reward.

A LION, A MOUSE AND A CAT

Once, there was a strong and mighty lion that lived in a cave atop a mountain. When he was asleep one day. A mouse came out from the hole and began to nibble his mane.

The lion was sleeping and this activity disturbed him. He woke up. The mouse ran away. The lion got an idea and brought a cat. He fed the cat well and left her loose in his cave. The cat stood guard and did not let the mouse trouble the lion. One day, the cat caught the mouse and threw him far away.

The lion was now free from the troubling mouse. He was relieved. The cat had no use for him. He stopped caring for the cat and feeding her.

Then the other mice started troubling the lion in the same way. The lion asked the cat to be on guard. The cat did not help him and left the cave.

Moral: Show gratitude to get help again.

THE BEAR AND THE GARDENER

Once, there was a mountain Bear who lived in a forest cave. The bear felt lonely and said to himself, "I must go and look for some friends."

The bear reached near a garden. After a while, he saw, from afar, a gardener who also lived alone. The bear was excited to find a friend. However, he was afraid that the gardener would get scared of him. So, he put on a mask. The gardener mistook him for another man.

"Welcome to my home. I am a lonely man. It would be nice if you could stay with me," the gardener said. Both started living happily with each other. One day, the bear saw a beehive on a tree in the garden. He could not control his wish to taste the fresh honey and climbed up the tree and broke the hive. The angry bees attacked him and the gardener. The bear ran away to the forest!

Moral: You cannot hide your true self forever.

THE WEDDING OF THE MOUSE

Once, a learned hermit went to bathe in the river. While he bathed, a hawk flew over him. The hawk accidentally dropped a mouse it held in his claws. The mouse fell into the hermit's hands. He turned the mouse into a girl. The girl grew up to be a learned and clever young woman. When she reached a marriageable age, the hermit asked her if she wanted to marry the Sun God. The girl refused. "The sun is too hot," she said. The girl also refused to marry the God of clouds. "He is too cold," she said. She refused to marry the God of Wind, calling him too fast. She refused to marry the God of Mountains too, as he was too rough. Finally, the hermit asked her, "Do you want to marry the king of mice?" The girl agreed. The hermit turned the girl back into a beautiful young mouse. The two mice got married.

Moral: Do not try to be something that you're not.

THE FOX AND THE GOAT

Once, a Fox slipped a fell into a well in the countryside. He tried to get out but he did not succeed. He saw a goat passing by. He got an idea. He called out to say hello to the goat.

The goat said, “What are you doing in a well?” The fox replied, “Don’t you know? There is going to be a great drought very soon. I jumped down here so that I have water by my side to drink.” The goat said, “Can I also come down then and we can share the water if it is alright?”.

The fox willingly agreed. The goat jumped down into the well with the fox. The fox immediately jumped on her back and managed to jump up to the edge of the well. “Good-bye, goat,” said the fox to the goat and ran away. The goat was now stuck inside the well.

Moral: Do not just blindly trust anyone without thinking.

THE DOG AND THE SHADOW

Once, there was a dog that had a piece of meat in his mouth. On his way home, he crossed a wooden bridge on a brook. As he started to cross it, he looked into the water of the brook and found a dog holding a piece of meat. He did not know that he is looking at his own reflection in the water.

The dog got greedy and opened his mouth to snap and scare the dog in the water. He wanted that piece of meat too. As he did that, the piece of meat in his mouth fell out and down into the brook.

The dog realized his foolishness and had to go back home without any meat. He decided never to be greedy again and keep his food safe.

Moral: Be careful of losing something you have for something that may not exist.

THE EAGLE AND THE BEETLE

A beetle was a very good friend of a hare. One day, the eagle wanted to capture the hare. The beetle requested the eagle to spare the hare. But the eagle did not listen and captured the hare under her claws. The beetle was very angry. He flew to the eagle's nest and rolled down all her eggs.

Next year, the eagle built a nest high in the mountains. But the beetle found it and destroyed the eggs again.

This happened year after year, till the eagle begged the beetle to spare her eggs. The beetle agreed on the condition that she will spare her friend, the hare and never hunt in their land again.

The eagle flew away and kept her promise.

Moral: Even the weakest may find means to avenge a wrong deed.

THE LION AND THE OTHER ANIMALS

One day, the King of the Forest, the lion called a meeting of the animals to give each one a responsibility in the upcoming picnic. He said to the elephant, "You carry all the required things on your back."

Then he told the bear, "Be prepared to bring anything that is needed." The lion said to the fox, "Your task is to find all the interesting spots." Then, he called the monkey and told him, "Take care that all should be amused by your tricks." While all the animals waited for their turn, one of them said, "What will the hare and the donkey do? "The donkey will be the trumpeter and the hare will make the announcement."

In this way, the wise King got all the animals involved in work.

Moral: Everyone has a talent to display.

THE GOAT AND THE DONKEY

A goat and a donkey lived on the same farm in the countryside. The goat had to work daily to find his own food. He saw that the donkey had an easy life as the farmer fed him well.

The goat got jealous. He did not acknowledge that the donkey worked very hard. He thought that if the donkey stopped working then the farmer will not give him food. Then the donkey will also have to search for his food. So, one day, he pushed him into a large pit. The donkey's leg broke. He was now not able to work.

The farmer showed the donkey to a doctor. The doctor said, "Give the donkey some goat soup every day and he will get well."

When the goat heard this, he ran away from the farm.

Moral: Do not aim for other's share.

THE FOOLISH MONKEY AND THE KING

There was once a king, and he had a very foolish pet monkey. The king loved his monkey a lot and trusted him. The monkey accompanied the king everywhere and lived in the king's room. One afternoon, the king was taking a nap. The monkey sat by the side of the king and fanned him. Suddenly, a fly came and sat on the king's nose. The foolish monkey was angry and did not want the king's

sleep to get disturbed. He tried to shoo away the fly. The fly kept flying away but returned to sit on the king's nose. Frustrated, the foolish monkey took the sword and tried to hit the fly. In his attempt, he accidentally hit the king's nose and hurt him. The king got angry and sent the monkey away.

Moral: A fool can never be of any help.

THE DONKEY AND HIS SHADOW

There was a traveller who hired a donkey to carry him on his journey to a distant place. It was a very hot day. The traveller sought to rest on the way and took shelter in the shadow of the donkey. On the way, he met another man who was looking for shelter.

As the shadow was big enough to give shelter and coolness to only one person, both of them started to fight.

The traveller said, "This is my donkey and I cannot share his shadow." As they both fought, the donkey got an opportunity to move away to go and sit under a tree himself for shade.

Moral: In quarrelling about petty issues, we often lose the substance.

THE LEOPARD AND THE SHEPHERDS

Once a leopard was near a village searching for food. There was a big pit there. He fell into it. A shepherd saw the leopard in the pit. He called the other shepherd and said, “Look a leopard fell into the pit.” The other shepherds were shocked and in fear pelted him with stones.

But some kind shepherds stopped them. So, the leopard was left alive. When he recovered from his wounds, he climbed out of the pit.

After a few days, he went to the village and scared all the families of the cruel shepherds who had pelted stones on him. After that day, the shepherds were never unkind to any animal again.

Moral: Never be unkind to animals.

THE EAGLE AND THE WOODCUTTER

A kind-hearted woodcutter once rescued an eagle from a trap. Sometime later, the woodcutter had climbed on a steep hill to cut wood. There he got stuck, and couldn't come down. He sat on a rock, waiting for some help to come. Suddenly, the eagle he had rescued came flying down towards him. In another moment, the eagle flew away with his hat. The woodcutter became angry and started to chase the eagle. After some time, he found the way to get down the hill. "Oh, so this is why you took my hat. You wanted me to run behind you and find the way. Thank you so much, my friend," the woodcutter said to the eagle.

Moral: Kindness will always get great rewards.

Tales from Panchatantra

Book-8

DREAMLAND PUBLICATIONS
J-128, Kirti Nagar, New Delhi -110 015, India
Tel : +91-11-2510 6050, 2543 5657
E-mail : dreamland@dreamlandpublications.com
Shop online at www.dreamlandpublications.com
Follow us on www.instagram.com/dreamland.publications

THE MICE AND THE OWL

Once, there lived an owl on a tree. He was a wise owl. He would pick his food in the forest and fly back home to enjoy it on his tree. One day, the other birds asked the owl, "How do you find food so easily?"

The owl told them, "I was flying one day when I saw the half chopped-down bark of a tree. It was full of insects and mice. When I tried to catch the mice, some of them ran away too quickly. So, I began to feed the mice with wheat, every day. The mice became fat and healthy. They became lazy and did not search for food. They waited for me every day to bring wheat grains."

So, the owl took them food and captured them one by one as food.

Moral: Greed will always lead you to your doom.

THE POTTER AND THE SCAR

A poor potter lived in a small village. One day, he fell into a ditch. He got hurt. The wound left a scar on his forehead. When the potter moved to another village, he had to find work.

He got work in the king's court telling lies about his scar. The king saw the scar on the potter's face. The king thought the potter to be a soldier. He treated the potter with respect and made him a commander.

In the following months, the kingdom was attacked by the enemies. The king asked the potter to lead the army. The potter told the king the truth about how he got the scar. The potter left the kingdom.

Moral: Never judge a person by his or her appearance.

THE GOLDEN ANTELOPE

Long ago, a gardener looked after the royal garden.

The gardener noticed a golden antelope grazing near the royal garden.

One day the king saw the golden antelope and was attracted by the antelope's beauty when he saw him at the corner of the royal garden one day.

"Can you catch that magnificent antelope?" The king asked the gardener.

"Yes, your Majesty!" said the gardener. If I had a little honey, I would bring him right into the palace," the gardener replied.

The next day, the gardener approached the antelope, offered him some sweetened grass, and brought him to the palace.

The gardener swiftly locked the entrance after the antelope was inside the palace, and the antelope began to shiver with fear at the sight of so many men.

The king felt sad and said, "There is nothing more disgusting in the world than to be trapped due to greed," he said, ordering the gardener to immediately release the animal.

Moral: Greed and lust are bad for all.

THE WITTY VILLAGER

Long ago, there was a wise man who lived in a village. He was taking his goat, lion, and a bundle of grass to another village.

The villager came across a large river while travelling. He found a little boat. The boat was so small; he could only carry one thing at a time while crossing the river.

"If I take the bundle of grass with me, the lion will eat the goat, and if I take the lion with me, the goat will eat the grass in my absence," the villager thought.

He thought of a plan and smiled. He crossed the river with the goat, leaving the lion and the bundle of grass behind.

The villager left the bundle of grass behind this time and took the lion with him. He crossed the river again, dropped the lion, and returned with the goat, ensuring that the lion could not harm the goat.

The villager returned with the goat to the spot where the bundle of grass had been left. He took the grass bundle this time and left the goat behind. The goat was now alone at the river bank.

The villager left the grass bundle with the lion after crossing the river and sailed back to get the goat. The witty villager crossed the river with the goat, lion, and bundle of grass in this way.

Moral: With wisdom, you can handle any situation.

THE PEACOCK AND THE FOX

A long time ago, in a forest, there lived a fox. He observed a lovely peacock sitting on a branch of a tree.

"How long should I keep looking for food?" The fox wondered, cunning by nature.

"Hello friend, why are you sitting up there on the tree?" The fox said to the peacock, using his plan in a pleased manner. "Did you hear the fantastic news?"

"What news?" The peacock enquired quietly.

"You know, today at an animal meeting, it was decided that animals and birds would no longer kill each other for food," the fox said.

The peacock exclaimed, "You mean the king lion, tigers, and leopards will begin eating grass from today?" The peacock continued, outwitting the fox.

Come down, we'll go to our king together and ask him to explain this point," the cunning fox suggested.

"Dear friend, we don't need to go there," the peacock said with a smile. I see some of your friends approaching this tree."

The fox was taken aback and asked, "Who are they?"

The peacock answered, "Hounds."

"Hounds?" the fox cried out in terror and he ran fast towards the hills. "Yes! But, who knows, maybe the hounds haven't heard about this meeting," the fox said as he ran away into the dense forest.

Moral: The trickster is also tricked at times.

THE FROGS IN MILK

Once upon a time, there were two frogs and they comfortably lived together in a tiny marsh.

They saw a grasshopper flying over a milk bucket. The frogs hopped up to the edge of the pail to capture the grasshopper with their long sticky tongues. The grasshopper, however, flew away, and the frogs splashed into the milk pail.

The pail had been half-filled with fresh milk. The frogs couldn't reach the top of the bucket because the milk level was too low and they couldn't get out since the sides of the pail were too high.

Both frogs kicked swam in circles until one of them became exhausted and slid to the bottom of the pail, his nose filled with milk.

The second frog, on the other hand, refused to give up. With its tiny feet, he kicked and battered the milk and the milk began to thicken.

Finally, the milk thickened to a point where it formed a ball of butter.

The frog leapt to his feet and skidded along the harder surface until he reached the pail's edge, and he hopped and jumped out of the bucket from there.

Moral: Never give up hope and keep trying.

THE HORSE AND THE DONKEY

There was once a washerman who had a donkey and a horse. The donkey put in a lot of effort for his master.

The donkey used to take clothes from the washerman's home to the pond. The horse occasionally took the washerman to the market.

Once the donkey was carrying a heavy burden and the donkey's back ached. "Brother!" he cried out to the horse. I'm tired from the weight, please share a portion of it with me."

"Why should I?" The horse neighed. The proud horse proceeded on his path, but the pitiful donkey continued to go slowly.

As the day proceeded, the temperature began to rise. The donkey fainted on the ground, and the washerman offered the donkey some water. Then he loaded the entire load of garments on to the back of the horse.

"I should have taken half of the burden when the donkey requested me," the horse realised. The horse had to carry the entire weight till they reached the market. The horse repented its arrogance.

Moral: Always be courteous to others and offer help when required.

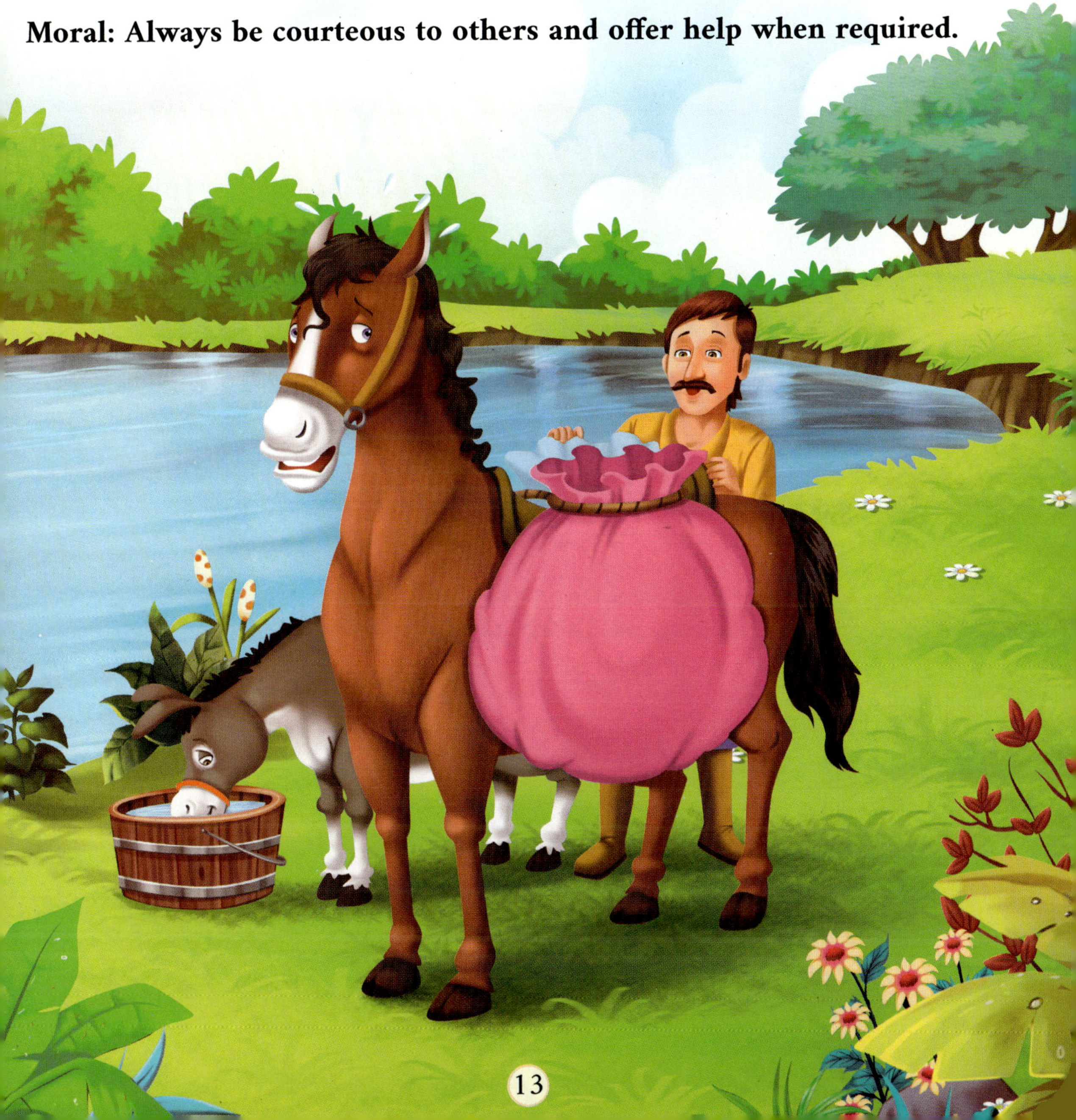

THE SWALLOW AND THE CROW

There was a very proud swallow that had beautiful colourful feathers. One day, the crow approached the swallow as it sat perched on a tree. The swallow looked at the crow and thought, "The crow looks so ugly with black feathers." He admired his beautiful feathers.

The swallow got a chance to talk and said, "You are black and your tail is so short." The crow said, "Yes, but I can fly about easily." The swallow replied, "I can also fly with my beautiful feathers and long tail gracefully." The crow reminded the swallow that her feathers were falling off and then she started shivering in the cold. The swallow felt bad because the crow never lost his feathers and was always warm in winters too. The swallow stopped being proud.

Moral: Never feel proud.

THE BIRD CATCHER AND THE CRICKET

One day, a bird catcher went to the forest. He wanted to catch a special beautiful bird. He heard a strange sound that was like music. He looked around for the bird.

"Maybe it is not even a bird and an even more beautiful creature that I can catch." He crept towards the sound. He ignored all the birds flying in the area. He tossed his net to catch the creature. He was shocked. It was a little cricket in his net. He realized his mistake. To catch the strange creature, he had let so many birds go. The cricket came out of the net because it was so tiny and flew away.

Moral: Do not lose the small prize by chasing a big prize.

THE HERMIT AND THE MOUSE

Once, in the olden days, a hermit took care of a temple in a small village. There was a mouse in that temple. This mouse stole the hermit's food kept in an earthen pot hung from the ceiling. The hermit was not able to get rid of this mouse.

Finally, the hermit sought his friend's advice. The friend advised him to find and destroy the food reserves of the mouse. The hermit made a search and found the hidden stock of the mouse and threw it away.

Without the stock of food, the mouse became weak and was unable to jump to the roof to get more food from the hermit's earthen pot. The hermit caught the mouse and threw it away.

Moral: Strike at the enemy's source of strength to defeat him.

Tales from Panchatantra

Book-9

DREAMLAND PUBLICATIONS

J-128, Kirti Nagar, New Delhi -110 015, India

Tel : +91-11-2510 6050, 2543 5657

E-mail : dreamland@dreamlandpublications.com

Shop online at www.dreamlandpublications.com

Follow us on www.instagram.com/dreamland.publications

THE TRUTHFUL DEER

A hunter once attacked a deer drinking water by a river. Surprised to see the arrow, the deer requested the hunter saying, "Sir, please don't kill me yet. Let me meet my family once before I die." The hunter did not believe the deer, so he followed the deer to his home. On reaching, he saw the deer meeting his wife and children. When the deer told them about the hunter, the deer family turned towards the hunter saying, "We are a family who cannot live without each other. Please kill us too." Seeing their love and bond as a family, the hunter lets them go free. "Your family love has taught me a great lesson. I will never kill any animal again," said the hunter.

Moral: Never harm any animal, care for them.

THE LION AND THE WOODCUTTER

Once, a lion lived in a thick forest, with two good friends, a crow, and a jackal. A woodcutter was chopping wood one day, he heard a sound. Swinging around, he saw a lion ready to spring upon him. The woodcutter addressed the lion as the King of the forest, and invited it to a meal cooked by his wife! He said that if the lion ate those vegetables, it would stop eating flesh!

The hungry lion relished the tasty vegetables. The woodcutter invited the lion to eat with him daily, but not tell anyone. One day, the woodcutter saw the lion coming with a crow and a jackal. The woodcutter asked the lion to leave as the lion had broken his promise and called his friends. The lion repented at having lost a good friend.

Moral: Don't break a promise made to a friend.

THE HARE AND HIS EARS

Once the lion was hurt by the horns of a goat that ran past him. The lion was quite angry. He commanded all the animals of the forest, to get their horns removed. The command frightened the animals that had horns.

They decided to leave the jungle. The hare was very restless at night. He thought that he had long ears and the lion might command all animals to give up their ears. He had an uneasy sleep. The next morning, he saw the shadow of his ears. His ears looked like sharp long horns. He shouted, "My ears have become horns by magic. I will leave this forest." The hare left the forest with the other horned animals.

Moral: Stay alert but do not go by assumptions.

THE WOLF AND THE LEAN DOG

One day, a wolf met a lean dog. He went closer to the dog but the dog kept going backward. The dog said, "I am just skin and bones. You will get nothing by catching me. In a few days, my master has a wedding feast for his daughter. I will grow fat and heavy eating rich food. Then you catch me." The wolf agreed. After some days the wolf returned and found the dog in the yard. He was fitter and healthier. He told the dog that he had come to take him away. "Open the gate." The dog said, "I shall be delighted. I'll come out as soon as the Porter opens the gate." Porter was a very huge dog. The wolf made off as fast as his legs could carry him.

Moral: Do not believe false promises.

THE UNGRATEFUL MOUSE

Once, there was a sage who lived in a forest. One day, a cat was chasing a mouse. The mouse went to the sage and asked for protection. The sage changed the mouse into a cat. Now, the other cat ran away in fear. Soon, a fox started to chase the mouse-cat. This time, the sage turned the mouse-cat into a tiger. The fox also ran away.

The mouse-cat began to enjoy a lot of powers as the tiger. He troubled the animals and frightened them. One day, he thought worriedly, "What if the sage turns me into a mouse again?" He decided to prevent this and kill the sage. The sage had magical powers so he came to know about it. The mouse-tiger went to kill the sage. But the sage turned the mouse-tiger back to a mouse and shooed him away.

Moral: Never be ungrateful.

THE COWS AND THE LION

Once, four cows lived in a meadow near a forest. They were good friends and were always together. No one managed to break their friendship. They always grazed together in the meadow and slept together. So, the lions and the tigers could not attack them as they had sharp horns too. One day a lion got an idea. He decided to create a fight between the cows. He told lies to the cows, and they fought with each other. Now, each cow started to graze in a separate part of the meadow. The lion saw this and decided to use the opportunity to capture the cows one by one. He hid in the bushes and surprised the cows one at a time, and took them away to his den.

Moral: Unity is strength.

THE SNAKE AND THE ANTS

Once upon a time, in a forest, there lived a king cobra. He went to a massive tree and made his home there. However, there was an anthill near the tree's roots. This irritated the king cobra. He decided to destroy the ugly anthill and attacked it.

The ants were not afraid of the snake. Thousands of ants emerged from the anthill and began crawling over the body of the king cobra. They had quickly coated his entire body. They stung him all over, giving him excruciating pain.

King cobra attempted to shake the ants off but was unsuccessful. The snake could not bear it and ran away.

Moral: Pride always gives you a fall.

THE ROOSTER AND THE JEWEL

A long time ago a rooster was looking for food and scratching the ground. Suddenly he found a diamond and wondered what to do with it. He did not know what it is and was puzzled. The rooster was happy to see the shine of the diamond. The rooster found it too hard and could not eat it.

Looking at the diamond he thought, “This gem may be very costly, but not for me. A single grain of corn will be more useful to me than this jewel which I cannot put to any use. The rooster just left it on the ground and began searching for food again.

Moral: No precious gem can replace the significance of food.

THE MONKEY AND THE WEDGE

Once upon a time, a merchant once planned to construct a temple close to his home. He used a large number of masons and carpenters to complete the project.

When the masons and carpenters went for lunch one day, a swarm of monkeys came down to the building site and began jumping around and playing with the tools.

A partially sawed log of wood was lying in a corner. The monkey was interested to learn what kind of tool it was.

He stretched his legs out on both sides of the log and began inspecting the wedge.

The monkey then grabbed the wedge and began pulling it out of the rift from the wooden log.

The wedge was finally removed and the split wood portions firmly snapped together, crushing the monkey's tail in the process. He shouted out in agony.

The masons and carpenters saved the monkey but his tail was permanently cut off.

Moral: We must not try activities that are unrelated to us.

THE THIEF, THE SAGE, AND THE DEMON

A wealthy merchant was unhappy to see the plight of a poor sage and donated calves to him so that he never went hungry. The sage was thankful, and soon with good care, the calves turned to be strong bullocks. The sage used his bullocks to plough the field and earn a livelihood. One night, a demon and a thief came to his house and saw his bullocks. They began to fight over the bullocks, and each of them wanted the bullocks. The sage woke up from sleep and saw both of them. He chanted a few holy mantras, and the demon ran away. Then the sage chased away the thief as well.

Moral: Fighting never gets you any results.

THE LION'S BAD BREATH

Once, the lioness told the lion that he had bad breath. This really upset the lion and he sent for his three counsellors — the Sheep, the Wolf and the Fox.

He asked the Sheep, "Tell me honestly, do you think my breath is bad?" The Sheep replied, "To be honest, yes you smell very bad from the mouth." The lion got so angry that he sent the sheep away.

Then the lion asked the Wolf. "Hey, is my breath bad?" The Wolf said, "You are the king of the forest. How can you have a bad breath? In fact, I think your breath is like the sweet scent of flowers." "Liar!" roared the Lion and he banished the Wolf from his kingdom.

He now turned to his third counsellor, "Fox, is my breath bad?" The Fox said, "Your Majesty, forgive me. I have such a nasty cold that I cannot smell a thing!"

Moral: Act wisely to save yourself.

THE FOX AND THE STORK

Long ago, there lived a crafty fox and a good-natured stork in a jungle. One day, the fox saw the stork in the jungle. Looking at his long beak, the fox decided to play a nasty prank on the stork. He invited the stork for dinner.

The stork accepted the invitation and reached fox's house. The fox served soup in two flat plates. The stork's beak was too long and pointy to eat the soup from the flat plate. Feeling sad, the stork quietly left whereas the fox enjoyed both the food and the prank.

One week later, the stork invited the fox for dinner. When the fox arrived, the stork served soup in long thin necked jars. The fox tried his best but could only lick the rim of the jar. This time, the stork enjoyed the delicious soup. The fox realised his mistake and apologised for his behaviour.

Moral: Never make fun of anyone.

THE MONKEY AND THE CAMEL

Once, there was a big party in the forest to honour King lion. It was his birthday. All the animals attended the party and requested the monkey to dance. The monkey was graceful and light, and he did one dance after another. The animals clapped in joy. The party was going very well. Seeing the monkey get so much praise, the camel felt envious. He also wanted the attention that the monkey was getting. So, he raised his hind legs and started to dance. As he kicked around while dancing, he hit many animals with his heavy hoofs. The animals were upset. Together they shouted at him and told him to stop.

Moral: Do not try to copy others.

THE MICE AND THE WEASELS

The weasels and the mice were rivals and were always fighting with each other. In every battle, the mice lost the battle to the weasels. After each battle, the weasels ate many mice and celebrated their victory. One day, the mice had a council meeting. They made a large army and appointed commanders and generals to lead them in the next battle. The new leaders wore feathers as ornaments. The mice were ready and sent a war challenge to the weasels. The weasels attacked the mice army. The mice fought hard, but the weasels took away the feathers of the generals and commanders. The mice ran into tiny holes to escape being caught. The weasels won the battle once more. The mice decided to keep away and never fight the weasels again.

Moral: Greatness has its penalties.

Tales from Panchatantra

Book-10

DREAMLAND PUBLICATIONS
J-128, Kirti Nagar, New Delhi -110 015, India
Tel : +91-11-2510 6050, 2543 5657
E-mail : dreamland@dreamlandpublications.com
Shop online at www.dreamlandpublications.com
Follow us on www.instagram.com/dreamland.publications

THE FOX AND THE EAGLE

Once, there lived an eagle and a fox who were neighbours and best friends too. The eagle built its nest on the branches of the tall tree, whereas the fox lived in the hollow of the same tree.

As time went by the eagle and the fox had children. Every day in the morning, the fox and the eagle would go hunting and bring food for their children and come back before evening.

Once it so happened that the eagle could not get any prey and it came back empty-handed. In the nest, her brood was chirping endlessly because they were feeling hungry. The fox's cubs were waiting for the fox at the entrance of the liar under the tree. The eagle did not know what to do to satisfy the hunger of its kids and it swooped down low and picked up one of the fox's cubs.

Just at the same moment the fox came back and seeing what the eagle had done shouted, "What are you doing my friend? Give back my cub, have you forgotten about our friendship?"

The eagle did not listen to the fox's cries. So, the fox rushed towards the nearby meadow and lit some dry bush from the burning cogon grass. The fox brought the bush to the tree.

The fox showed the burning bush and said to the eagle, "Return my cub, or else I will burn down this tree to ashes." The eagle's offsprings were very small and if the tree was burnt they would not be able to save themselves. So, the eagle came down and returned the cub to the fox. The fox immediately left the tree with its cubs and went deep into the forest never to be seen again.

Moral: Never break trust in friendship.

THE DOG, ROOSTER AND THE FOX

Once there were two friends a rooster and a dog who lived in a farmyard. One day they wanted to see the world outside their farmyard. They wanted to explore the things outside the farmyard so they decided to leave the farm.

The rooster awoke with the first rays of light. He stood tip-toes on the branch of the tree and proudly crowed. The rooster awoke a fox in the forest not far away. The fox said in an evil tone, "I can't express how delighted I am to see you here."

The rooster asked the fox, "How is that even possible?"

"My friend, our king Lion has announced that all animals, birds, and other creatures in this forest should not kill one another."

The rooster exclaimed, "O' wonderful!" Will you be so kind as to walk to the bottom of the tree and inform my friend who is resting there?"

The fox rushed to the tree's hollow, believing there were more roosters below.

On seeing a dog in the hollow of the tree, the cunning fox immediately began running to the forest. The fox said in a loud tone while fleeing, "I am afraid that your friend may not have heard about the king lion's new policy of peace."

Moral: The cunning can also be out-witted.

THE CAT AND THE CROW

Once upon a time, there lived a cat and a crow. They were close friends who spent a lot of time together. They lived at the edge of the forest.

Once, the crow noticed a leopard approaching the two when they were together. The crow flew to a high branch. The cat asked, "Dear friend, won't you help me? You are the only one who has the ability to save me."

The crow flew over and came across a bunch of herders accompanied by their pets. He flew down almost to the ground before flying directly at the dogs and catching their attention.

The crow then flew straight towards the leopard and the dogs followed the crow in the hope of catching him.

The dogs barked loudly as they approached the leopard. The crow was flying high in the sky. When the leopard heard the dogs' bark, he rushed back to the forest, leaving the cat behind. The crow succeeded in rescuing his friend, the cat.

Moral: A friend in need is a friend indeed.

THE KING AND HIS SONS

Once upon a time, there was a king who had three sons. A thought occurred to the king one day. He called his sons and told them, “I am giving each of one of you a seed that you will plant in a pot.” After some time, I’ll see who has the best plant.

The next king will be the one with the most beautiful plant.” All three of them received the seeds from the king.

The king called his sons with their plants after sometime. Two of his sons with plants in their pots declared happily, “Look, father, how beautiful our plants are!”

The youngest son said, “I tried everything I could, but no plant grew in my pot.”

“No! The seeds I gave you and your brothers were dead and useless, so you should not be sorry,” said the king. Your brothers have deceived me. They sowed new seeds in their pots when they noticed their plants were not growing.”

“The plants they have are from different seeds,” said the king.

However, you were truthful and honest with me, and one of the most crucial qualities of a king is honesty. As a result, my beloved son, you will be the future king,” the king added.

Moral: Honesty is the best policy.

THREE FISHES

Dolphins, whales, and other little colourful fish used to live in a sea a long time ago. All of the marine animals were quite nice to the dolphins.

One day, the Whales harmed the fishes, who were friends of the Dolphins. The Dolphins became enraged and began battling the Whales. All the Dolphins assembled to fight with the massive Whales.

The battle had reached its heights; a Sprat appeared out of nowhere and attempted to speak to them. "Why are you fighting?" he asked. I think I can solve the problem if you let me in."

One of the Dolphins was very wise. She realised the Sprat was taking advantage of the fight between the Whales and the Dolphins and so she asked others to ignore the Sprat.

The Dolphins fought on and each of them was victorious.

As his plan to rule over the fish failed, the Sprat became irritated and left. He realised that the Dolphins were smart. They were well aware that a third party's interference would be harmful to everyone.

Moral: Never let an outsider into your personal life.

THE NAUGHTY LAMB

Once upon a time, a tiny lamb and his mother goat lived together. The young lamb wandered into the forest one day. He was excited to see the big trees and vibrant flowers. He then realised he was lost in the forest and he said to himself, “I fear I’ve gone away from home. Mother is going to be furious with me.”

There was a wolf hiding behind a tree, whom the young lamb could not see. The wolf stealthily moved towards the lamb.

When the wolf moved, the small lamb noticed him and cried out, “Help... Help...” “A small animal like you should not come to this deadly forest,” the wolf said.

The mischievous lamb gathered his bravery and ran away as quickly as he could. The wolf followed him furiously.

Meanwhile, the mother goat was concerned because she hadn't seen her lamb for a long time. She spotted the small lamb racing towards her and a wolf chasing him as she approached the forest.

The mother goat promptly chased the wolf away with her big horns. "I hope you have now learned that the forest is not the place for goats like us," the mother goat remarked as she led the small lamb back to their house.

Moral: Listen to an elder's advice.

THE PEACOCK AND THE CRANE

A long time ago, a proud peacock lived beside a lake. A crane arrived to stay beside the lake one day. The peacock greeted him warmly and became his friend. The peacock then stretched his beautiful tail in the sun to impress the crane.

In the brilliant sunlight, the peacock's colourful feathers looked stunning. "My dear friend, take a look at my feathers," the proud peacock exclaimed. Your feathers, on the other hand, are as grey as dust. You don't have as lovely feathers as I do."

The crane understood the peacock's tone and silently heard his remarks. A hunter passed by the lake the next day. When the crane saw the hunter approaching, it took off quickly.

The peacock, who was engrossed in his reflection in the lake's water, found it extremely difficult to flee and was quickly captured in the hunter's net.

When the crane saw this, he flew down quickly and used his beak to attack the hunter. The hunter was gravely injured by the crane's attack and fled leaving the peacock in the net behind.

"Friend, your feathers are indeed extremely attractive, but I can soar high and defend myself with these and that is enough for me." The peacock acknowledged his error and apologised.

Moral: It is better to be useful than being only beautiful.

THE BEES AND THE BEETLES

There was a huge beehive on a tall tree in the forest. The bees had stored a lot of honey in it. A colony of beetles lived in the tree trunk of an old tree nearby. The bees and the beetles were good friends.

One day, the bees invited the beetles for dinner. They offered them their best and sweetest honey. The beetles did not like the taste of honey and did not eat it. They thanked the bees and flew away.

The next day, the beetles invited the bees for lunch. They served the bees a plate of dung. The bees did not touch it. They said thank you and flew away.

Moral: People can have different likes and dislikes, but still they can be good friends.